Yes, No,
Little Hippo

Do you know . . .

A library is a magic castle with many Word Windows in it?

What is a Word Window?

If you answered, "A book," you're right.

A book is a Word Window because the words, and the pictures that tell about the words, let you look and see many things. Books are your windows to the wide, wide world around you.

CHILDRENS PRESS
HARDCOVER EDITION
ISBN 0-516-05724-3

CHILDRENS PRESS
PAPERBACK EDITION
ISBN 0-516-45724-1

Library of Congress Cataloging in Publication Data

Moncure, Jane Belk.
  Yes, no, Little Hippo.

  (Magic castle readers)
  Summary: After experiencing several falls and
bumps, Little Hippo discovers how to play safely
and have fun without the danger of accidents.
  [1. Hippopotamus—Fiction.   2. Safety—Fiction.
3. Play—Fiction] I. Gohman, Vera Kennedy, 1922-
ill.   II. Title.   III. Series: Moncure, Jane Belk.
Magic castle readers.
PZ7.M739Ye   1988   [E]   87-21211
ISBN 0-89565-411-3

Yes, No,
Little Hippo

by Jane Belk Moncure
illustrated by Vera K. Gohman

Created by

Distributed by CHILDRENS PRESS®
Chicago, Illinois

The Library —
A Magic Castle

Come to the magic castle
When you are growing tall.
Rows upon rows of Word Windows
Line every single wall.
They reach up high,
As high as the sky,
And you want to open them all.
For every time you open one,
A new adventure has begun.

Beth opened a Word Window. Here is what she read.

One night Little Hippo said, "I will jump
on my bed." He jumped very high.

"No, no, Little Hippo," said his sister.
"It is not safe to play that way."

But little Hippo went on jumping. He jumped higher and higher until . . .

he jumped off the bed and fell . . .

on the floor.

Mama Hippo picked him up. "No, no, Little Hippo," she said. "Beds are not for jumping. Beds are for sleeping."

She kissed the bump on his head. And
she tucked Little Hippo safely in bed.

The next day Little Hippo said, "I will climb on a chair. I will climb very high."

His brother came by.

"No, no, Little Hippo," he said.
"It is not safe to play that way."

13

But Little Hippo went on climbing. He climbed higher and higher until . . .

the chair tipped over.

Little Hippo fell . . .

down

Plop

on the floor.

Mama Hippo picked him up. "No, no, Little Hippo," she said.

"Chairs are not made for climbing. Chairs are made for sitting." She kissed the bump and sent him outside to play.

Little Hippo saw a friend.

"Hi, Little Hippo," said his friend.
"Let's ride our bikes."

"I can ride very fast," said Little Hippo.

He hopped on his bike and went
very fast

d
o
w
n

the hill.

"No, no, Little Hippo," said his friend.
"It is not safe to play that way."

But Little Hippo went faster and
faster down the hill. He went
so fast he took a spill.

Papa Hippo picked him up. "No, no, Little Hippo," Papa said. "Riding too fast is not a safe way to play."

"All I ever hear is no, no," said Little Hippo. "Is there anything I can play so that you can say, 'Yes, yes, that's the way'?"

"Yes," said Papa Hippo. "Yes, yes."
And off they went to the park.

Did Little Hippo jump at the park?

Yes. Yes. He jumped rope instead
of jumping on his bed.

Did he climb at the park?

Yes. Yes. He climbed very high on a jungle gym instead of on a chair.

Then Papa said, "Let's go for a boat ride in the park."

Did Little Hippo put on a life jacket?
Yes, he did.

"We can do one more thing," Papa said.
"Let's ride in the cars," said Little Hippo.

Did he fasten his seat belt? Yes, he did.

28

And when it was time to go home, Little
Hippo said, "Fasten *your* seat belt, Papa."

Did Little Hippo have fun at the park?
Can you guess?

That night Little Hippo  made a safety book. You can  make one too.

My Safety Book

✓ Yes

42 Elm Street

I know my street address.

✓ Yes

I know my phone number so I can call home.

✓ Yes

I don't play with matches.

✓ Yes

I ask Mom before I taste any food or drink.

30

I buckle my seat belt in the car.

I stay away from strangers.

I look both ways and listen before I cross the street.

I obey safety rules at home and school.

I don't go into the swimming pool alone.

I pick up toys on stairs so nobody falls.

31